The Big Storm

by Penny Anderson
illustrated by
Seymour Fleishman

Published by The Dandelion House
A Division of The Child's World

Distributed by Scripture Press Publications, Wheaton, Illinois 60187.

Library of Congress Cataloging in Publication Data

Anderson, Penny S.
  The big storm.

  Summary: Four Christians stranded by a snowstorm keep
a prayerful vigil with a farmwoman waiting for her
husband to return home.
    [1. Storms—Fiction.   2. Christian life—Fiction]
I. Fleishman, Seymour, ill.   II. Title.
PZ7.A54875Bi   [E]   82-7433
ISBN 0-89693-206-0   AACR2

Published by The Dandelion House, A Division of The Child's World, Inc.
© 1982 SP Publications, Inc. All rights reserved. Printed in U.S.A.

1 2 3 4 5 6 7 8 9 10 11 12 R 89 88 87 86 85 84 83 82

The Big Storm

"Watch that ice!" Dad shouted.

Jenny woke up with a start. She had fallen asleep in the back seat on the way home from Grandma's.

"Oh, Lord, please help me!" Mom cried as she struggled with the wheel. The car seemed to skate into space. Then it plunged off the shoulder of the road and into a snowbank. It stopped with a sickening crunch.

Jenny's seat belt cut into her stomach. She began to cry.

"Are you all right, Jenny?" Mom asked.

"I'm all right," Jenny said, rubbing away her tears. "What happened?"

"We ran off the road," Dad said. "The storm's getting worse. The temperature has dropped. Where the road was wet, it is now covered with ice. I think we're the only people out." He turned to Mom. "See if you can back out."

Mom tried. The engine roared. The tires spun. The car did not move. There was the smell of hot rubber.

"Here, let me try it," Dad said. They changed places. Dad tried to inch the car forward and then back. But the car did not move. He tried over and over again. The car settled deeper in the snow.

In the beam of one headlight, Jenny could see swirling snow. The wind was blowing in great gusts, rocking the car and piling the snow against the windshield. Jenny tried to look out the other windows but couldn't see anything.

"We can't get out," Dad said.

Jenny gulped. Her throat ached.

"What will we do?" Mom asked. "Maybe nobody will find us . . ." Her voice shook.

"Hey, let's not think like that," Dad said. "I'd better get out and look around."

"Don't leave us, Dave!"

"I'll be right back."

"You can't see. You'll get lost."

"We can't sit here and freeze."

"What about the heater?"

"Look at the gas, Elaine. We're almost out. But . . . before I leave, let's pray. We need God's help. Let's trust Him."

Jenny closed her eyes as Dad prayed aloud. Then quickly Dad opened the door, stepped into a deep drift, and slammed the door. He disappeared into a sea of snow.

"Don't cry, Mom," Jenny said, feeling a little braver after Dad's prayer. "It's not your fault . . ."

"I know."

"Dad will be right back. You'll see."

"I know, Jenny," Mom said, peering into the storm. She and Jenny sat in silence. The cold crept into the car, numbing their hands and feet. "Pull on your mittens, Jenny, and zip up your jacket."

"I already did."

"And your boots . . . are they fastened?"

"I'm fastening them now."

The door flew open and a blast of icy air and snow filled the car.

"Come on," Dad said. "I can see a light far across the field. Let's go!"

Jenny pulled up the hood on her parka. She was glad she had worn her ski suit. She climbed out into the snow.

"Take my hand, Jenny," Mom said as she grabbed Dad's arm. The three of them blindly straggled up the steep snow bank and across the icy road. Far in the distance was the glow of a farmer's yard light. Holding onto each other, they plodded through the snow toward it.

Jenny's cheeks were numb. Her hands and feet felt wooden as she stumbled up the porch steps. Dad knocked, then knocked again. They could hear someone inside. Mom held Jenny tight against her. The porch light came on and a woman stared out. "What do you want?" she called out.

"Can you let us in? Our car ran off the road," Dad replied.

After a minute that seemed like an hour, the woman unlocked the door, released the chain, and let them in. They stood dripping snow on her kitchen floor as the warmth of the room washed over them.

"Thank you, Lord, that we're safe from the storm," Jenny whispered.

"We're the Scotts," Dad said. "I'm Dave. This is my wife, Elaine, and our daughter, Jenny. We're sorry to bother you like this . . ."

"I'm Mrs. Johnson — Nellie Johnson," the woman replied, smoothing back her grey hair. She pushed her glasses up more firmly on her nose. "I was a bit afraid to let you in. You have to be careful these days. But I know you can die out in a storm like this." She paused. "You look safe enough. Come, take off your wet things. I'll make some hot chocolate."

She looked at Jenny. "Would you like to help me?"

Soon they were sitting around the kitchen table, warming their stiff hands around mugs of cocoa.

Mrs. Johnson said her husband, Frank, had gone into town early in the afternoon. "He's not back yet," she said. "That's why the yard light was on . . . so he could find his way in the storm."

"If your yard light hadn't been on, we would have frozen to death. We couldn't see the house lights at all through the blowing snow," Dad replied. "Thank God you had it on!"

Suddenly a huge gust of wind hit the house, rattling the shutters. The lights went out. Jenny nestled closer to Mom.

"Oh, dear, what else will happen?" Mrs. Johnson moaned. "Now where are those candles?" Within seconds Mrs. Johnson lighted a big red candle and placed it in the middle of the table.

"Will your husband try to come home in this blizzard?" Mom asked.

"I'm afraid he will. He knows how scared I am of storms. I tried to call his sister to see if he had stopped there, but my phone's gone dead. I hope he's all right." Mrs. Johnson's eyes filled with tears. Jenny felt sorry for her.

Just as their eyes were getting used to the candlelight, something fell onto the porch, hitting the door with a crash.

"What's that?" Mom gasped.

"Frank! I'll bet it's Frank!" Mrs. Johnson cried, flinging open the door. She seemed to forget all about being careful. Then she screamed. "It's not Frank! Help!"

Dad rushed to the door as a young man with dark hair stumbled in. The young man carried a guitar case.

Sinking into a chair, he pulled off his gloves and cap. He was still breathing hard, and his hands were shaking.

"I thought it was Frank. I thought my prayers were answered. I thought it was Frank . . ." Mrs. Johnson was crying softly. Mom put her arms around her.

The young man sat with his head in his hands. He seemed to be talking to the floor. "I can't believe it . . . I can't believe it. . . . It took me an hour to get the last few miles. And then my van turned over. I couldn't see a thing when I rescued my guitar and crawled out. Then I saw your yard light. But I thought I might freeze before I got to the light. And then the light went out just before I got here."

Mrs. Johnson handed him a cup of hot chocolate. "These are the Scotts," she said. "Their car ran off the road a little while ago. I'm Nellie Johnson. I thought you were my husband coming home."

"I'm Joe Martin. I've been playing and singing at a

youth rally in Blooming Grove. I was trying to get back to the university.''

"We were trying to get home," Dad said. "We saw the yard light too. We're all lucky to be here."

"I don't think it was luck," Joe said, shaking his head. "The Lord was with me. I prayed as I haven't since I was a little kid. I was sure I couldn't take another step when I fell onto your front porch, Mrs. Johnson."

"I've been praying that Mr. Johnson will get home safely," Jenny said.

"Do you really think your husband is out in the storm?" Joe asked.

Mrs. Johnson nodded and began to cry again. Jenny walked over and put her arms around her. Joe watched helplessly for a minute, then reached for his guitar. He took it out of the case carefully. Soon soft music filled the candle-lighted room.

"Do you know any choruses?" Jenny asked. Joe began to sing. Jenny joined in. One by one the others pulled chairs into a little circle around them and listened.

They sang songs of praise and joy. When they sang "Kum Ba Yah," Joe explained that it meant, "Come By Here." When they sang the verse, *"Someone's cryin', Lord,"* Jenny looked around the circle. Everyone had tears. Everyone was feeling sorry for Mrs. Johnson, whose husband was somewhere in the storm.

"*Someone's prayin', Lord*" was next. Joe stopped playing. He took hold of Mrs. Johnson's hand on one side and Jenny's on the other. Soon the group was holding hands, forming a circle of prayer.

It was a long night. The wind howled, driving the snow against the windows. A shutter banged somewhere on an upstairs window. The house creaked and groaned. The group huddled closer together in the kitchen, where the stove worked to keep them almost warm. Of course, when the electricity had gone off, so had the furnace.

Shivering, Jenny looked around. She was thankful for Mom and Dad, Mrs. Johnson and Joe. She was thankful for this farmhouse with the funny old kitchen stove. She was thankful for the food Mrs. Johnson provided. Jenny was more thankful than she had ever been in her whole life.

Later, Mrs. Johnson brought blankets and quilts. The group wrapped up in them and dozed now and then. Sometimes they talked, and sometimes they sang.

It was hours later when, through a blur of sleep, Jenny saw the sun beaming through the kitchen window. She looked around, remembering where she was. She realized there wasn't a sound anywhere. The storm was over.

Mom and Dad, Mrs. Johnson, and Joe were drinking coffee. In the distance Jenny heard a rumble.

"What's that?" she asked, untangling herself from the quilt.

"I don't know. It seems to be coming from the road," said Joe. Mrs. Johnson hurried through the cold house to the front windows. Jenny followed her and looked out.

The sun was dazzling. The snow sparkled like diamonds. It almost blinded Jenny. Squinting, she could see a great plume of snow billow into the air like smoke.

"It's the snowplow from town!" Mrs. Johnson exclaimed. They watched as the plow rumbled slowly forward, then stopped. When it was almost to the house, Jenny saw a man get out and wave to the plow as it churned forward again. The man headed for the house, struggling and falling through the drifts that were almost waist-deep.

Mrs. Johnson gave a choked cry. Wrapping a coat around her shoulders, she forced open the front door and stepped out on the snow-covered porch. "Frank! Frank!" she called.

The man stopped and looked toward the porch. He waved his arms and plunged toward her.

When the two came inside, Mr. Johnson was surprised to see a crowd standing there. But he was more surprised when Jenny ran up to him and said, "I prayed that you would get home safely." Slowly a smile crept across Mr. Johnson's broad face.

Watching him, Jenny knew that she would never forget this night. She knew she would always remember the big storm, Mrs. Johnson, Joe, the old kitchen stove, the candle, the songs of praise. Most of all, she would always remember that God hears and answers prayer.